Where Is the Rocket?

Harriet Ziefert

Illustrations by Barroux

BLUE APPLE

Blasting off, circling 'round,
Over, under, up and down.

Upside down? Right side up?

As far as the stars?

As near as your pocket?

Where is the rocket?

near

far

on

Where are we?

Where are we going?

outside

inside

Where are we now?

up...

and on the left

What's on your left?

What's on your right?

down...

and on the right

over

under

Are we there yet?

through...

Where to now?

mid

What's in the middle?

Is this the middle of the book?

dle

corner

Now where?

to the **top**

at the **bottom**

Where to next?

behind

Where are we?

in front

upside down

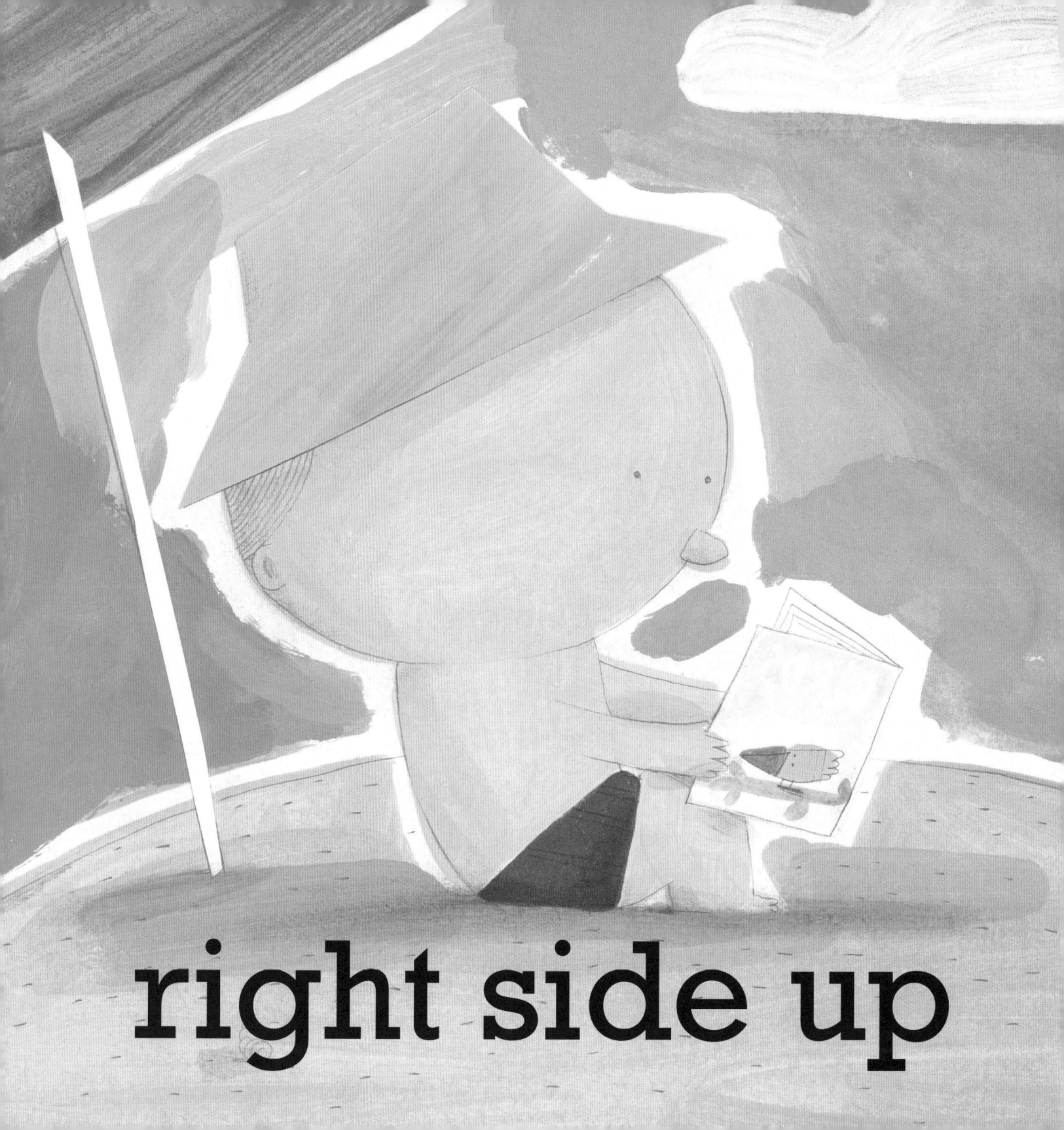

right side up

almost there...

Where?

HERE!

And where are you?

What's in front of you?
What's behind you?

What's to your right?
What's to your left?

What's near to you?
What's far from you?

What's above your head?
What's below your feet?

What's outside?
What's inside?

What's in the corner?
What's beyond?